Trapped in Battle Royale
Book Six

ATTACK FROM TILTED TOWERS

AN UNOFFICIAL NOVEL OF FORTNITE

Devin Hunter

Sky Pony Press
New York

CHAPTER 1

After an easy run through Greasy Grove, Grey glanced at the number of people left in the battle. There were thirty players even though only the third storm was upon them. Any minute Tae Min would say what he usually said—it was time for him to eliminate himself. Grey hated that Tae Min wouldn't play with them for longer, but if Grey wanted all his friends to go home, he had to accept it.

"Well, it's about time—" Tae Min started.

"You got out?" Finn finished for him. "Here, I'll help you this time!"

Finn threw an impulse grenade at Tae Min, who was running ahead of them by just enough so that no one else took the hit. Tae Min went

1

flying over the edge of the mountain. The drop was a long way down, and Grey watched in shock as Tae Min hit the bottom.

Tae Min had a great fall.

"Why you . . ." Tae Min said, but then he began to laugh.

Everyone else joined in. Playing with Tae Min had made *Fortnite: Battle Royale* fun again despite being stuck in virtual reality.

"I want to eliminate Tae Min next battle!" Kiri said. "Revenge for all those head shots he landed on me."

"If we find impulse grenades," Tae Min said, "I'm all yours, Kiri."

"Sweet as, mate." Kiri let out a pretend evil laugh.

"We should have thought of this sooner," Finn said. "That elimination credit could help your ranks if we end up in ties with Lam's squad."

"True," Grey said. "We'll rotate eliminating Tae Min then."

"This is what I get for training you?" Tae Min said jokingly.

It hadn't been long since Tae Min had joined their squad and began to train them. Grey had worried they couldn't get every Victory Royale like Tae Min wanted, but so far either Grey's squad or Ben and Tristan's duo had taken the wins as planned.

"Head through Snobby," Tae Min said.

"Okay." Grey, Finn, and Kiri headed northwest, since the storm was pushing them that direction. It looked like the safe zone circle would be shrinking between Haunted Hills and Pleasant Park, in a mountainous area that would be precarious to fight around. "It's a good thing we got Lam's squad down early. She'd be all over those mountains."

"She'd already have her base outfitted," Finn said. "But Zach and Hui Yin are still up. Vlad and Yuri, too."

"No slacking," Tae Min said. "Ben and Tristan are counting on you for backup in the end."

Ben and Tristan had made an alliance with Grey's squad once Hazel had decided to leave. And even though they couldn't all fit in one group, it had worked out well. Tae Min had taught Ben and Tristan how to hide until the end of the game. It was boring, but it had paid off.

Snobby Shores was untouched when Grey's squad arrived there. "Should we loot? We have a minute until the storm starts to close, and we could use more mats."

"Go for it," Tae Min said. "Expect some fights soon, though. Some may rotate from Tilted thinking the same thing."

"I'll keep a lookout," Kiri said as she ran into the closest house. Grey moved a bit deeper into the ritzy houses that made up Snobby Shores. There was a time when he worried about Kiri being on her own, but she had come a long way since their first days in the game. Kiri wasn't a scared noob anymore—she was a sniper who was almost as good as Tae Min, and she also had improved her building enough to compete with the best.

Grey broke down furniture and opened chests. So far, there hadn't been any weapons better than what he had, but as he popped open the next one, a legendary rocket launcher glowed before him. "Got an orange rocket launcher."

"Awesome," Finn said. "I found a chug jug and more small shields, but no better weapons. Who can carry the shields?"

"I will," Grey said as he glanced at his mini-map to see where Finn's icon was.

"Ooo! A legendary sniper!" Kiri said. "We're looking flash now, ay?"

"So flash," Finn said.

"The storm is closing in three seconds," Tae

Min said. "You better get your flash selves to the safe zone."

Grey met Finn and picked up the shields, and then they all began to move again. The purple storm began to fill up more of Grey's screen, and he knew they wouldn't be able to outrun it. It wouldn't have been too bad, but then gunfire sounded.

"Ack!" Finn said as his shield dropped to half.

Grey built several walls to guard them while he tried to spot where the shots came from. With the storm upon them, they didn't have time for a fight.

"Directly to the east!" Kiri said as she built a wall and ramp. She already had her sniper out and took a shot. "One is white."

That meant she had hit one for enough damage to burn off their shield, which showed blue numbers when it was hit.

"It's two," Tae Min announced. "If they push, it's probably Zach and Hui Yin. If they box to heal, it's Vlad and Yuri."

Tae Min had most of the competition read down to the tiniest detail. He knew how they moved and what their play styles were. He knew where his enemies liked to land and what weapons they favored. And, of course, he knew how to counter them all.

Sure enough, one of the players used a bounce pad. They flew through the air, aiming at Finn, who they had already damaged.

They all fought back, but Finn still took enough damage to go down.

The storm enveloped them at that moment, and Grey frantically tried to get their enemies down before Finn was fully eliminated. He couldn't go down now . . . They still had twenty people left in the battle.

"The no-skin is one hit!" Tae Min yelled. "Focus!"

Grey turned his attention to the player Tae Min called out, and he landed one hit with his hunting rifle.

You eliminated Zach.

Grey took a hard hit that melted his shield, and he threw up a wall to protect himself. The storm was already ticking away at his health, but the same was true for all of them.

"Get somewhere safe, Finn!" Kiri yelled. Her health wasn't doing so hot, either, but surely they could get Hui Yin down with the storm's help.

"There's no way," Finn said. "Hui Yin's gonna thirst me."

Hui Yin eliminated Finn by head shot.

"She's low," Tae Min said. "Stop hiding and get her."

Grey mustered his courage. One good hit from Hui Yin's shotgun would take him out, but if he could hit her first . . . He built a few ramps to get the high ground. Hui Yin was doing the same, and he used one of his own walls to block her path. She began to move to the right, and Grey took the shot.

You eliminated Hui Yin.

"Now run," Tae Min said. "Wasted too much on that."

"I know," Grey said as he and Kiri began their frantic run to the safe zone. "I'm sorry, Finn. Maybe we shouldn't have hit Snobby."

"It's all good," Finn said. "Still top twenty. I have a decent average."

Grey didn't reply. He felt too guilty. He hated leaving a friend behind, especially his real-life best friend. Finn needed good ranks more than anyone since he came into the game halfway through the season and had fewer games to average out.

It wouldn't feel right if Grey couldn't get all of his friends home by the end of the season.

CHAPTER 2

Ben and Tristan took the win for that battle, and then they all showed up in the battle warehouse for the end of the day. The Admin appeared with her usual smile. "This concludes Day Fifty-Five of Battles. There are now five days remaining in the season. No reports have been submitted. You may now use the practice area until mandatory rest time."

Five days.

Grey looked at the rankings on the battle warehouse wall. That last game had dropped Zach and Hui Yin even more, and now it was Kiri sitting in the fifth rank. Grey was in the sixth. Ben and Tristan were in the ninth and tenth ranks with Finn in eleventh.

"Oh my gosh, fifth!" Kiri put her hands over her mouth as she stared at the board. If today had been the last day of battles, Kiri would be going home.

Grey was happy for her, and he smiled. "One down, four to go."

"We got this!" Kiri said as she held up her hand for a high five.

Grey gave her one.

"Nice, Kiri!" Ben said as he, Tristan, and Finn joined them. "You're locked in!"

"No one is locked in," Lam said as she walked past them with her squad. Hazel followed her new squad leader, but she glanced at Grey as she passed. He could see the fear in Hazel's eyes, even though she currently sat in the fourth rank. Another day of victories for Grey's squad would probably knock Hazel out of that spot and Kiri into it.

"Time to practice," Grey said.

Tae Min had already left the building. He had them meeting at the ghost town still, since they were tirelessly working on their close-quarters combat. Grey panicked every day, wondering if it would be the day Tae Min announced that they were ready for Tilted Towers. But so far it hadn't happened.

Every day that passed, fewer people were spotted in the practice area. Today, as Grey passed through the cabin area, he spotted Hans's squad around the campfire. They had been pushed to the bottom of the top twenty. So, even they were giving up now with just five days left.

In another day, he wondered if only the top ten would be fighting for it. It made sense with so few games left and the ranks harder to achieve. But it made the games weirdly boring because they were so easy until the last ten or fifteen people. Maybe Grey's squad had gotten better, but he had a feeling most people were just messing around at this point.

"Did you see that the tomato man's head is gone?" someone said as Grey passed by. "I can't believe it! He was an icon."

"These rifts are so weird," another person replied. "There's one at the motel, too. They're showing up all over."

"I can't wait to see what happens next season!" chimed in a third person. "It's gonna be epic!"

Finn groaned. "Ugh! I wanna see what happens next season!"

"You will," Grey replied. "It will just be on a computer screen instead of here."

That didn't seem to make Finn feel better, because he rolled his eyes at Grey. "C'mon, you really think it'll be the same? One, it's super cool to see it in person. Two, the video game version isn't the same as the virtual reality, remember? If we get out, I could have missed everything already."

"*When* we get out," Grey said.

"Fine, 'when,'" Finn replied. "But it still sucks not to see what will happen."

"Maybe you'll miss some things," Kiri said as they entered the practice area, which looked abandoned in comparison to the crowd around the campfire. "But it's not like you won't be able to play *Fortnite*. In here, we are literally missing out on our lives. And we can't get that time back."

"Exactly," Ben said. "Trust me, you don't want to be in here for a year. I'd do anything to get a break at this point. Even for one day."

"Me too," Tristan said.

Finn didn't say anything to that, although it seemed like he had plenty to say that he was keeping to himself. Grey wanted to ask him about it, but Finn didn't like to talk feelings, especially in front of other people. Grey would have to find a chance to hang out with just Finn and see what was up.

After they stocked up on weapons and materials, Grey and his friends headed out to the ghost town to meet Tae Min. As they climbed over the hill, Grey was shocked to see what Tae Min was doing.

He was building Tilted Towers.

Not that he could make it exactly, but he had used metal to build the dimensions of the different towers. He had added all the details to each one he'd built to the point that Grey could recognize some of the infamous towers, like the castle tower, the clock tower, the construction site, and Grandma's house. Tae Min wasn't finished, and Grey could see him putting up walls for another building.

"Holy . . ." Ben said as they all stood there in shock.

"And here I thought I knew the map," Tristan said. "I could never rebuild it like this even though I've been here as long as Tae Min."

"This is crazy," Finn said. "And freaking awesome."

"We better get down there." Grey started walking. If Tae Min was putting so much work into their training, Grey wasn't about to waste that effort. They needed to use this replica as much as they could in the hours before mandatory rest, because after that it would be reset for the next day.

"There you are," Tae Min said as he stopped building for a moment. "It's not perfect, but this will help you get a feel for Tilted."

"You think?" Grey looked around in awe. "Do you need help?"

Tae Min shook his head. "Use the finished buildings to play hide-and-seek for now. Everyone solo. Try to get familiar with the layouts of the towers. If you break stuff just build it back. I'll call you when I'm done."

"Sounds good." Grey turned to everyone. "You heard him! Let's go!"

"You are all going down!" Finn said as he ran toward the castle tower.

"We'll see about that!" Ben called back as he ran after Finn.

Grey decided he'd take a look at the clock tower first. It was the size of a one-by-one structure and it went straight up. He opened the door at the bottom and looked up. There was a ceiling several stories high, but no stairs. He knew there was a balcony on top that usually had a chest or two, but this place seemed dangerous to land on. It could be easy to fall, and there wouldn't be much loot or materials.

As Grey walked back outside, he took several

shots. He looked up and spotted Finn at the top of the castle tower.

"Gotcha!" Finn yelled. "Try harder, Grey!"

"I'm looking around!" Grey said with a smile. He figured they would all take shots at him, but it was good aim practice for them. He needed to learn the layout of this place because Tae Min would eliminate himself, and Grey would be in charge after that. Of all the places on the island, Grey knew the least about Tilted Towers.

Grey chose to explore the construction site next. This building was interesting because it wasn't complete. There were holes in the floor and some unfinished walls. As he looked around from inside, he could see how vulnerable he'd be in this building.

In fact, he took no less than ten hits as he moved from floor to floor.

"You're miserable at hiding today," Kiri said as she met up with him in the castle tower.

"I'm *thinking* of hiding places," Grey said. "But I'm trying to memorize these buildings."

"Good, because we'll be going over chest locations now." Tae Min's voice came from behind. "And we need to discuss landing strategies. It's vital to have a plan right as you go in. There isn't a second to waste in Tilted Towers."

Grey nodded. "Let's do this."

Ben and Tristan met up with them in the castle tower, and Tae Min began his detailed training on loot in Tilted Towers. He showed them every possible chest spawn point in castle tower, and then he tested them to make sure they all had the locations memorized.

"This is mad," Kiri said. "We have to do this for every tower?"

"It's majorly important," Finn defended. "Getting a weapon is first priority in Tilted, and if you waste a second wandering, you might be eliminated right off because you didn't pick up the gun first."

"Exactly," Tae Min said. "Finn, your expertise here will be vital. You'll need to back up Kiri and Grey while they get the hang of this in battles."

Finn smiled confidently. "I will, don't worry."

"If we're hiding," Tristan said, "will this training help us at all?"

"Yes," Tae Min said. "Once we get this, I will switch squads like Grey suggested. I don't intend to hide with you guys—we will be fighting."

"Oh . . ." Ben squared his shoulders. He hadn't been paying much attention, but now he looked like he regretted that.

Tristan smiled. "Good. I'm dying of boredom in those hiding spots all battle."

Finn put his hand on Tristan's shoulder. "I feel ya, dude."

"Okay, back on task," Tae Min said. "I haven't built all of Tilted—I don't have the time—but these are the buildings we're memorizing tonight because this is where I want you to land tomorrow."

Grey's eyes went wide as fear shot down his spine. "Tomorrow?"

Tae Min nodded. "You're ready, combat-wise. After tonight, you'll be prepared on position-ing. We can't delay any longer. Landing in Tilted means more eliminations, and you might need those if your ranks tie with Lam's squad. They never get aggressive, so you'll outrank on eliminations."

"Right . . ." Grey took a deep breath, trying to convince himself that he was ready. He'd put in the work. He'd trained with the best people in this virtual reality version of *Fortnite*. There was no reason to be afraid of Tilted Towers anymore.

Or was there?

CHAPTER 3

Grey and his friends practiced right up until the end of the day. He had packed in as much information as he could about chest locations. Tae Min also taught them good positions for landing and they went over their close-quarters combat. It only made Grey feel slightly more confident to hit Tilted Towers tomorrow.

They had to run back to their cabins before the mandatory rest period. Everyone else was already in their beds as they dashed for their own resting places. Grey hopped into his bed just before the countdown ended.

The next day, Grey woke with a new surge of nerves. What if they were eliminated early in Tilted Towers? They couldn't afford to get a rank under the top five—ranking in the nineties or eighties for even one game would be disastrous. From everything Tae Min and Finn had said, it still seemed like it was impossible to predict how Tilted Towers would go.

"I need to clear my head," Grey said as he stood up from the bed. "Is that okay?"

"Sure," Tae Min said. "We'll be at the usual practice spot when you're ready."

Grey nodded and then headed to his favorite forest spot. He hadn't had as much time to think alone since Tae Min joined the squad, and he realized just how mentally fatigued he was as he leaned on the barrier deep in the forest.

He tried to push Tilted Towers out of his mind for a minute, instead focusing on why he had to do this. He needed to get home. It had been almost two months now. If he was in the real world, he'd be getting ready to go to seventh grade. His mom would probably be taking him shopping for new things, and he'd be trying to get in every last moment of fun he could before being stuck in class again.

It was funny how he *wanted* to be stuck in class instead of a game.

But classes ended. And it felt like this game

never did. So he wanted to go back to school. He wanted to see his family and friends. He wanted to eat food again and go to the real outdoors where he could feel the wind and rain and sun. And if he wanted all that, then he had to stop freaking out about landing in Tilted Towers.

"Hey, Pipsqueak." Hazel's voice cut through the silence. Grey was so deep in thought that Hazel startled him. "Sorry. I know you like your alone time."

"It's okay," Grey said, although he was leery about why Hazel might have come to see him. They hadn't really spoken much since she left the squad, and there hadn't been any trolling like there was before she joined them. Even with all the friends he had, he still missed her. "What's up?"

"Not much." Hazel sat down next to him and looked up at the tree branches. Tears began to form in her eyes. "You guys are coming for my spot home. Feels like I made the wrong choice."

A lump formed in Grey's throat. He genuinely felt bad for Hazel, but he didn't know what to do to help. "I told you we'd make it, but you wouldn't believe me."

"I know," Hazel said as she wiped her eyes.

"It just sucks. How was I supposed to know Tae Min would swoop in? You never said anything."

"I didn't know he would," Grey replied.

Hazel leaned forward and put her arms on her knees. "You know, that's just the sort of luck that sums up my entire life. And by luck, I mean I have none. Now it might cost me everything."

The guilt Grey felt weighed down on him. Now he knew where this was going—Hazel was about to beg him for a spot in the top five. And he didn't know how to tell her he couldn't make that sort of decision. "Maybe your family cares more about you than you think they do. It might be okay."

Hazel's tears began to fall faster. "You're right, they might. But that doesn't mean they have the money to pay the hospital bills. Either their care or their money will run out at some point, sooner rather than later. I'd rather not have to face what happens when either one is gone."

"There are six of us," Grey said. "I want you to go home. I wish every single person stuck here could go home. But what do you want me to do? I can't replace anyone."

"I know, but . . ." Hazel had more to say, but she kept it to herself until Grey couldn't stand it.

"But what?" he asked.

"Can't *you* stay?" Hazel's question came out in a whisper. "You're friends with Tae Min. You could easily get home next season. Your family will wait for you for sure, and you know it."

Grey was so shocked by what she was asking him to do that he couldn't speak immediately. She was technically right, but it took a lot of guts to ask him if he'd give up his spot for her. And the truth was that he didn't want to. He had sacrificed a lot to help his friends already, but giving up his spot . . .

"Hazel, I can't." Grey looked down at his hands, feeling like the most selfish person ever born. "I've worked so hard. I've helped everyone I could. It's not fair to ask me to do that. Would you ask any of the others? Or are you just asking me because you know how much I care about people?"

"You're right, I don't think anyone else would even consider it," Hazel admitted. "I had to try."

"I wish you hadn't," Grey said as he stood up. He didn't want to be angry at Hazel. He knew she was desperate. "I already felt guilty enough about it."

"I'm sorry," Hazel said.

"I gotta go." Grey walked away, even though part of him still wanted to help Hazel. This was not the relaxing moment alone he wanted, and now he was more worked up than before. Was that her plan? To sabotage him for Lam's squad? He hoped she hadn't stooped that low, but at this point in the competition, any crazy plot was possible.

Once he met up with his friends, they all gave him a concerned look. So he hadn't shrugged off his emotions as well as he hoped.

"You don't look so good, mate," Kiri said. "Did something happen?"

He didn't want to tell them, but he couldn't keep this pent up inside. "Hazel asked me to give up my spot in the top five for her."

"Seriously?" Ben said in surprise. "Who does that?"

"Someone desperate," Tae Min said.

Finn's brows were pinched with worry more than anyone else. "And what did you say to her? You're not gonna do it, are you?"

Grey shook his head. "I really wish I could help her, but I can't give that up."

"Of course you can't," Tristan chimed in.

"But I still feel bad," Grey admitted. "I wish

we could all go home, you know? It's not that I don't want her to be top five. I just can't give up my spot. That doesn't make me a jerk, does it?"

"She's messing with your focus," Tae Min said. "My bet is that was her real intention—to throw you off your game so you don't play well today."

Finn shot Tae Min a glare. "C'mon, Hazel isn't like that."

"She was a straight-up troll to us when the season started," Tristan pointed out. "She could definitely be doing that. You didn't know her before."

"People can change," Finn said. "Hazel is honest, and she would ask because she wants to go home just like the rest of you. There doesn't have to be another motive all the time!"

"That is fair," Tae Min said. "But regardless of her intent, we are being distracted. Can we put this behind us and focus?"

Everyone agreed, and Tae Min went over their plans for the day. He was still trying to fit in all the tactics he wanted them to remember when they were teleported to the battle warehouse.

It was time to see if all their hard work would pay off.

CHAPTER 4

The Battle Bus had a perfect path for landing in Tilted Towers. In fact, it would fly directly over it. This did not excite Grey because it meant there would probably be a lot of other players landing there. Even if those players weren't as skilled, anyone could get lucky with enough chaos thrown into a fight.

"Grey, I can feel you stressing even without seeing your face," Tae Min said.

"Sorry," Grey replied.

"Land on your assigned building, get a weapon, and do what I taught you," Tae Min said. "Call out if you get in trouble. I will be there for every game because we're landing there first."

"C'mon, Grey," Kiri said. "We all know you can do it, so you gotta believe it, too."

"Okay, okay." Grey tried to steady himself. He was prepared. He could do this.

"Time to jump!" Tae Min left the bus first. Finn, Grey, and Kiri all jumped right after. Since they were all landing in different buildings, they were already spread out in the air.

Grey wanted to close his eyes so he couldn't see how many people were landing with them at Tilted Towers, but he had to see where he was going. His heart pounded as he counted no less than fifteen other players landing at the island's hottest spot. Even if they were all less skilled and there to play for fun, it would still be a feat to make it out alive.

Fights started before Grey had even landed on his designated building—Grandma's house—that was on the outskirts of the area. It was a smaller blue building that could easily be targeted from the other bigger ones. Tae Min wanted Grey there because he believed he could handle the fire better than Finn or Kiri.

Grey hoped Tae Min was right.

As he landed on Grandma's roof, someone else did as well. There was one basic AR with ammo there, and Grey rushed for it. If he didn't get it, then he may as well accept early elimination.

Luckily, it showed up in his inventory instead of in the other player's. Grey opened fire as the other player ran off the side of the building. Grey chased, determined to eliminate that player before they got a weapon. Once they were gone, then Grey could focus on getting more loot.

The player tried to run inside the front door, but Grey fired at them until a notification popped up in his vision:

You knocked down Selena.

"Lorenzo's squad is here," Grey said. They weren't a top squad, but they weren't bad either. It wouldn't hurt to put everyone on alert. "They might come for me after this."

"We got your back," Tae Min said.

Grey fired a few more shots at the bunny avatar crawling toward the hiding spot under the staircase.

You eliminated Selena.

Selena didn't have any materials or items yet, so nothing popped out as she disappeared. Grey moved through the first story of Grandma's house, breaking furniture with his pickaxe and picking up all the loot he found. This time he had plenty of weapons to pick from, but there wasn't a single shield or bandage to be found. Grey didn't like having only one hundred health even in normal battles, but it definitely didn't feel like enough in Tilted Towers.

"Anyone have extra shields?" Grey asked as he opened the last chest in his building. There was a purple scar and a trap, which was great, but still no healing.

"I do," Kiri said. She was in the castle tower. Though a lot of people liked to land there, Tae Min picked that tower for Kiri because it was a central sniper position. "Come to me. Top floor."

Tae Min eliminated Sydney.

Kiri eliminated Diana.

"Okay." Grey worried about getting to her in one piece. He only had two hundred wood, and the castle tower was not only down the street but at the top. He could get hit from multiple directions as he made the trek. But he had to, so he broke down a wall for extra brick and began the run past the clock tower and through the street.

Finn eliminated Dan.

Shots came Grey's way almost immediately, and he lost a third of his health. He built walls and ceilings to protect himself as he made his way into the construction site, which was right next to the castle tower. Grey knew Finn would be there and was grateful Tae Min had made a thorough plan. "Finn, I need backup. Coming to you."

"Just picked up a med kit for ya," Finn said. "In the basement."

"I'm bringing a friend." Grey jumped and built to protect himself as he ran. He still took one more hit, bringing his health down to just thirty. One more hit would take him out.

Grey placed a trap as he ran down the stairs to the basement. He didn't hear it go off, but it made the players chasing him stop to destroy it.

"Here, dude," Finn said. "Hurry."

Grey grabbed the med kit as Finn built walls around them. The med kit took ten seconds to use, but as the enemy opened fire on them, it felt like it took forever. Finn kept the walls up as the SMG fire broke them down, and finally Grey's health popped up to full. "Got it."

"Dropping wall," Finn said.

Grey switched to his shotgun and aimed for the player. When the wall went down, he and Finn fired at the same time.

You knocked down Lorenzo.

"Thirst him," Tae Min said. "I got the other two in his squad knocked."

"Yes, sir!" Finn fired again.

Finn eliminated Lorenzo.

Tae Min eliminated Coco.

Tae Min eliminated Julio.

"That was too close," Grey said as he grabbed the small shields Lorenzo had been carrying. He used them both to get to fifty shields. "Sorry about that, guys."

"You're good, don't worry," Kiri said. "My building is clear, but there's two in the big red brick next to castle. One moving to the building south of clock tower. Another in the office building."

"I'll get the office," Tae Min said.

"We'll go big brick," Finn said.

Things were beginning to quiet down— Grey could tell just by the lack of gunfire in comparison to when he first landed. He and Finn made their way out of the construction site and across the street to the building Kiri called out. Grey made sure to look at the ceiling when he opened the door, and sure enough, there was a trap there. Tae Min had warned them to keep an eye on traps in Tilted Towers—with all the chaos it was easy to not pay attention and get spiked.

Finn shot down the trap and they moved inside. With all of the training they had, it wasn't hard to find their opponents and take them out. Tae Min eliminated the one he was after, and by the time they started searching for the last player, she was gone.

"We'll run into her later," Tae Min said. "Loot everything before the storm comes."

Grey's squad already had pretty good loot, but there could always be better stuff in an unchecked chest. They moved through the remaining buildings, but some of them were still foreign to Grey. He followed Finn, who knew Tilted Towers nearly as well as Tae Min.

"There's one here, too," Finn said as he used his pickaxe to break the ground outside near a park area.

Grey could hear the shimmering sound of the chest, but he never would have guessed it was underground. Once it broke, Grey and Finn jumped down to open the glowing, yellow chest. Out popped a stack of C4 and some other items they didn't need. Grey sacrificed his blue sniper for the C4. "We have four C4 now."

"Nice," Tae Min said. "Let's get moving."

After the fast-paced play in Tilted Towers, the rest of the game didn't feel nearly as stressful. Facing one squad or duo didn't seem scary after what they'd survived. Grey liked that side effect of landing in a high-risk zone.

The storm circle would be over the south part of the map this battle, so Grey's squad built up to the mountain looking over Tilted Towers. They could get to Shifty Shafts from there. He hoped they would find someone in the mines because they already had everything they needed to fight. He worried he wouldn't have many materials, but he had more than he expected.

"Stop," Tae Min directed before they even got close to Shifty Shafts. Tae Min held up his sniper so he could use the scope to get a closer look. "Hazel's there. Time to give Lam's squad an early loss."

Normally Grey would be happy about that, but after what Hazel asked him to do, he could only feel guilty.

Finn sighed. "I guess we have to take the shots, huh?"

"I will," Kiri said as she equipped her purple sniper. She took aim, and even though it was still hundreds of yards away, a notification read: *Kiri knocked down Hazel.*

"Push now!" Tae Min said as he let more shots fly.

"Bouncer?" Finn asked.

"Do it," Tae Min said as he laid down a wall for Finn to place it on. Tae Min took it without hesitation. He didn't shoot at Hazel but at someone even farther away in the houses across from the mine.

Grey and Finn went next. As Grey flew through the air, he spotted one of Hazel's squad members on their way to revive her. He unloaded his AR firing at the person, but they didn't get knocked down before they boxed themselves in. "The one on the road is white," said Grey.

"I have the one in the house," Tae Min said.

"Taking the snipe on Hazel," Kiri announced.

Kiri eliminated Hazel by head shot.

"Ouch," Finn said. "She won't be happy about that."

"I know," Kiri replied. "But I need the rest of my mates in the top five. I can't be the only one."

Grey pushed the guy in the box with Finn, and they both used their SMGs to burn down any walls the guy built. When the enemy tried to build up ramps, Grey didn't waste his materials, instead shooting down the ramps. The guy fell, and Finn was ready and waiting.

Finn knocked down Trevor.

"Two down," Finn said as he thirsted Trevor on the spot. "Two to go."

"Not for long," Tae Min said. "Hurry, these two are trying to run."

"Impulse grenade coming at Finn and Grey!" Kiri announced now that she had made her way down the mountain. She threw the grenade at Finn and Grey, and they went flying toward the houses. Since they were low to the ground, they wouldn't take fall damage, so Grey prepared himself for the chase. Lam and Pilar could not survive to late game—the lower their rank this game, the better.

"They're gonna launch pad," Tae Min said.

"No they won't!" Grey built up to the top of the house where a build battle had started. He could see the platform where Lam and Pilar were, and he threw C4 at it. The launch pad went down, but Grey exploded everything before Lam and Pilar could use it. They fell to the ground.

Grey eliminated Lam.

Grey eliminated Pilar.

Lam's squad was eliminated in the fifties for rank. It would definitely hurt their overall score, maybe even bump another of Grey's squad to the top five.

"Perfect," Tae Min said. "You can handle it from here, right, Grey?"

"Yeah," he said.

"I get to eliminate you! I have the impulse 'nades!" Kiri said.

After Tae Min had his customary "great fall," the rest of the battle wasn't much of a struggle. No one but Lam's squad could face them at their full force, and even then they didn't have much chance anymore.

Grey's squad took the Victory Royale easily, and when they appeared back in the battle warehouse, Grey immediately looked at the rankings on the wall. His heart sped up as he took in what he saw.

He was ranked number five.

Kiri was now four, and Hazel had fallen to six.

Grey had finally achieved what he had worked for the entire time he'd been stuck in virtual reality. He was in the top five. He could go home if he kept it for a handful of days. He couldn't help but smile as that truth sank in.

"Thanks a lot, Grey," Hazel said as she burst into tears and ran out of the warehouse.

Grey's elation vanished as he watched her go. It was hard to be happy for his own success when it came at the expense of a friend.

CHAPTER 5

While Hazel had run from the warehouse, her new squad was still there. They glared at Grey and his friends. This was swiftly becoming a battle between them alone, and it would be fierce.

Lam said, "Are you happy now?"

"I'm happy for myself and sad for Hazel," Grey said.

"You did that to her," Lam said. "Because you're a bunch of selfish kids who can't wait your turn. You know how much Hazel needs this."

"I've waited plenty of turns and never got moved up to the front of the line," Tristan said. "You know this isn't about waiting your turn—it's about *taking* your turn."

"Yeah," Ben said. "Don't guilt-trip Grey for doing exactly what you would do. Why don't you give up your spot for Hazel? Or are you selfish too?"

Lam glared at him, but she didn't jump at the chance to sacrifice her spot, either. Instead, she walked away with Trevor and Pilar. Grey hoped they would go and comfort Hazel, but he had a feeling they didn't care that much. It wouldn't be right for him to do it.

"I know that look," Finn said. "You're worried about Hazel."

Grey sighed. "Is that so wrong?"

Finn shook his head. "No. I'll go talk to her, okay? We both started in the squad at the same time, so we're buddies."

"Thanks," Grey said. Finn would be able to help. He and Hazel got along well—they had similar personalities. Though they bickered, they seemed to understand each other like they were siblings.

"You guys did well in Tilted," Tae Min said as if nothing happened. "Think you'll be okay if I squad with Ben and Tristan after a couple more battles?"

Grey nodded. "I don't have to land in Tilted, right?"

"No," Tae Min said. "I'll take Ben and Tristan there instead."

"Good." Grey had a feeling that after two more Tilted Towers landings, he would need a break from the fast-paced starts. "Practice?"

"Of course." Tae Min led them back to their usual practice area, and this time he built the twin apartments that were to the south of the construction site in Tilted Towers. They didn't have time to study more than that.

Finn showed up with only a few minutes before the next battle. He looked tired. Grey couldn't imagine what he talked to Hazel about for nearly an hour.

"Everything okay?" he asked his best friend.

Finn shrugged. "Not really. She's majorly upset you took her spot."

Grey frowned. "I feel horrible."

"Don't," Finn said as he put a hand on Grey's shoulder. "It'll work out however it works out. You can't control the Admin's rules."

"Exactly," Kiri said. "You aren't responsible for this, Grey. She shouldn't be mad at you—she should be mad at whoever made this place we're stuck in."

The next battle begins in thirty seconds!

"Everyone get your heads in the game," Tae Min said as they all prepared for the teleport. "This is the reality of making top five. If you want it, that means other people lose it. The end."

Grey tried his best to accept the truth of Tae Min's words. He knew this would be hard. He knew people would get hurt. He couldn't fix every bad thing about the game no matter how much he wanted to.

He and his squad appeared in the Battle Bus, and this time the bus's path wasn't as ideal for Tilted Towers. It was flying from south to north over the east side of the map.

"We're jumping early so we can get there," Tae Min said. "Right when the door opens."

Grey readied himself, though he was nervous they wouldn't land in their ideal places at Tilted Towers. "What do we do if we mess up the landing?"

"Well, don't mess up, but get a gun and make do if you land badly," Tae Min said. "At least hit a tower we've studied."

"Okay." The moment the bus's door opened, Grey and his squad leaped out. They were so high up he could see the entire island in his view. He tried to stick close to Tae Min for the time being, just so he could get the right height when he pulled out his glider to soar into Tilted Towers.

The only good thing about going to Tilted Towers from this bus path was that fewer people flew their direction. Instead of fifteen extra players, it looked like it would only be ten of them total. They could manage that.

Just as Grey feared, he was too low in the air to land at Grandma's house by the clock tower. He would be lucky to hit the twin apartments they had just studied instead.

"I'm gonna have to hit first floor of the castle," Kiri said.

"Same on construction," Finn said.

"Roof of twin here," Grey reported as his feet hit the flat black roof. He was right by a pistol and he grabbed it before breaking the roof. There was someone on the other side of the buildings doing the same thing—they would definitely meet inside. Grey had to hope he found better gear before they did.

He dropped right onto a chest and opened it. There was a gray shotgun, ammo, and small shields, but it was something. After drinking the shield potions, he broke down all the furniture and moved to the next room and the next. The deeper he moved inside, the louder the other player's footsteps grew. Grey wished he had a trap for extra protection, but so far he hadn't been that lucky.

Once Grey opened the next door, he found the enemy. He fired his shotgun out of instinct, and he hit the enemy for head shot damage. It wasn't enough, since the shotgun was only a basic one, but the girl had to be low on health. Instead of ducking behind the wall, he gambled and took some damage. But it paid off.

You eliminated Martine by head shot.

"Nice one, Grey!" Finn called over the comms.

"She had a purple scar, too. Sweet," Grey said as he picked up the loot. She also had bandages, but he hadn't taken enough damage to use them since they could only fill you up to seventy-five health.

"I'm gonna need backup," Finn said before Grey could loot the rest of the twin apartments. "There's three in here with me."

"On my way," Grey said.

"In the basement," Finn said. So much for this being an easier land in Tilted Towers. As Grey ran to help his best friend, Finn took a big chunk of damage. Grey wished his avatar could run faster, but he was stuck going the same speed as everyone else.

Finn's health bar turned red before Grey could even get in the building. "Don't come! There's no way . . ."

Jamar knocked down Finn.

"No!" Grey yelled. It was only the beginning of the game. If Finn was eliminated now, he'd take a ranking in the eighties for the game. Finn couldn't afford such a bad loss if they were to get him in the top five.

"They're gonna thirst," Finn said. "Don't come, Grey. I'm serious."

Jamar eliminated Finn by head shot.

"Oh no!" Kiri said. "Your ranking."

"Just think about yourselves for now," Finn said. "That's the luck of Tilted sometimes."

"We'll come and avenge you," Tae Min said. "They're the only ones left here anyway."

Grey didn't want to wait for Kiri and Tae Min, but he knew he should. So he crouched to walk quietly and found a place to wait. He could hear the footsteps of Hazel's old squad. Jamar, Sandhya, and Guang may not have been the top ten, but they were usually in the top thirty even now. Grey might have been angry, but he wasn't stupid enough to go in one versus three.

Grey spotted Tae Min building to the top of the construction site. Kiri broke out of the castle tower and built her own floors to meet Tae Min.

"They're first floor," Grey said as one of them walked right by his hiding spot. He took a deep breath and stood, shooting the player from behind. They spun around and shot back. Grey crouched under his natural cover to avoid the first hit, and then he built walls around himself.

He knew pretending to box in would be great bait for this squad.

Sure enough, they all showed up to try and eliminate him. Kiri and Tae Min pounced on the enemies from above, and they were finished.

"Good job, guys!" Finn said. "That'll teach them. You better win this one in my honor."

"We will," Kiri said.

The rest of the battle went smoothly, although Grey hated that Finn was out the entire time. Tae Min stayed with them longer than usual, only going out after they eliminated Lam's squad. That was right before they hit the top ten for the battle.

Grey and Kiri managed to pull off the Victory

Royale, but it didn't feel the same without Finn there with them.

With the battle finished, all of Grey's friends appeared back at their practice site. The duplicate twin apartment from Tilted Tower was still there, and they gathered in front of it.

"Sorry about that loss, Finn," Tae Min said. "We shouldn't have let that happen."

"Don't worry about it, seriously," Finn replied. "We're still doing great."

Tae Min nodded. "I'm gonna work on the next building. You guys keep on twin practice while I work. You good for me to switch squads next battle, Grey?"

Grey nodded. "Sure. Just give us the landing location and I can deal."

"Go for Lucky Landing," Tae Min said.

Tae Min switched squads and started building while the others practiced in the twin apartment. Soon enough, it was time for the third battle of the day. Everything went smoothly in Lucky Landing because Grey's squad was the only one there, but it was still strange not to have Tae Min around telling them what to do.

"It's quiet," Finn said as they ran up to Fatal Fields to get into the next storm circle. "Too quiet."

"Yeah," Kiri said.

Fatal Fields looked like it hadn't been touched. Grey kept an eye out as they looted some of it on their way, but he was paying more attention to the notifications of who was being eliminated. So far Tae Min, Ben, and Tristan must have been surviving in Tilted Towers because Grey only saw their names on the good side of the elimination announcements.

"Ah!" Finn yelled as he took damage out of nowhere. "Sniped!"

Grey began to build walls around himself while his teammates did the same thing. He peered through the slats and spotted the enemies pushing them. "Looks like two."

"Going in!" Finn yelled as he began ramping up aggressively.

"Wait!" Grey said. They had to be careful without Tae Min to back them up. While they had grown more skilled, Grey wasn't about to be overly confident.

More shots fired, and before Grey could even act, Finn's health bar went red again.

Vlad knocked down Finn.

"Shoot!" Finn yelled. "They didn't look like a top team."

"Push, Kiri!" Grey said as he aimed at the walls Vlad and Yuri had built to protect themselves. They were definitely going to eliminate Finn if Grey and Kiri didn't push hard—Grey couldn't let his friend take yet another low ranking.

"Using my minigun," Kiri said as the bullets began to fly nonstop.

Grey built higher to get above them, and he aimed for the player who wasn't rebuilding the walls. The yellow numbers showed on Grey's screen, indicating the head shot. The player built a roof, and Grey knew what would come next though he wanted desperately to stop it.

Vlad eliminated Finn.

"Sorry, man," Finn said. "My play is way off today."

With Finn gone, the players turned on Grey and Kiri. Vlad was already low, so Grey was able to get him down without much trouble. Yuri almost knocked Grey down, but Kiri came through with the relentless minigun fire.

In all the chaos, Grey only had time to look at the remaining players after Vlad and Yuri were eliminated. There were fifty players left. Another bad rank for Finn. Grey and Kiri were still able to get to the final four, and this time they gave the Victory Royale to Ben and Tristan.

When they got to the final battle of the day and Finn took yet another early elimination, Grey finally lost it.

"What is wrong with you?" he yelled over the comms. "You know better than to run into five players!"

"Sorry," Finn said. "I guess we're not that strong without Tae Min, are we?"

"You played better than this before he was ever in our squad," Grey said.

"Calm down, Grey," Kiri said. "Everyone has bad days. Getting mad at him won't help."

"He hasn't had a day like this since he got here!" Grey replied. "He came here a good player. It's almost like he's . . ."

That's when it clicked in Grey's mind. Finn wasn't just getting eliminated from bad luck or hard battles. Finn knew what he was doing—he was taking early losses on purpose.

And he started doing it after he talked to Hazel.

Finn was tanking his rank so Hazel could have the final spot in the top five.

"Are you gonna finish that thought, Grey?" Kiri asked as they backed out of the fight before they were eliminated like Finn.

"Never mind," Grey said. "Just focus on the game. You're right. I'm getting too worked up over this."

This wasn't the time to talk about what Finn was doing. Grey still had to do well, even if his friend was losing on purpose. Grey would have to confront Finn about it once the battle was over.

CHAPTER 6

When Grey and his squad appeared in the warehouse after the last battle of the day, Grey didn't even hear what the Admin was saying as he took in the rankings on the wall. Kiri and Grey had stayed in the top five, but Finn had gone down two ranks so that he was now behind Ben and Tristan. Hazel was still right behind Grey.

If Finn kept getting eliminated early . . . it wouldn't be long until the top five was out of reach for him.

Grey had to convince Finn to stop this before it was too late.

"Me and Finn gotta talk," Grey said the moment the Admin disappeared. He grabbed

Finn by the arm and dragged him out of the battle warehouse.

"Ow, ow, ow!" Finn cried as he squirmed out of Grey's grasp. "What the heck are you doing? Why are you so mad about one bad day?"

Grey pointed to the forest. "Not here."

"Fine." Finn stomped into the forest, and when they got to the barrier, he turned around on Grey. "Now will you tell me why you're being such a jerk?"

"How about you tell me why you're giving up your spot for Hazel?" Grey demanded.

Finn's eyes went wide. "Oh. You figured it out."

"Of course I did!" Grey threw his hands up in the air. "You made it completely obvious! All those bad games in a row. Throwing fights I know you could take solo if you wanted. Not sneaky at all."

Finn cringed. "I thought it was. I forget you're smart."

"I just don't get it," Grey said. "What did Hazel bribe you with? How could you try to give up your spot without even talking to me?"

"Because I knew you wouldn't listen!" Finn's voice burst out of him.

"I listen to you!" Grey replied.

Finn shook his head. "You hear my words, sure, but you haven't really taken in anything I've said this whole time. You think I want exactly what you want."

Grey's anger began to wane, replaced with a sense of fear. "I don't get what you're saying."

"I know." Finn let out a short, sad laugh. "You can tell I'm throwing battles, but you can't see all the hints I've given this entire month I've been here. I knew you'd be upset . . . so I've just been avoiding it. I figured if Hazel beat me out for the top five then it would be fine. We'd both get what we wanted without me having to face you."

A lump grew in Grey's throat as he began to connect the dots. "You don't want to go home."

"No, I don't," Finn said flatly. "I've told you a million times that I like being here. I like seeing all the events in person. I like fighting as if I'm really in the game. But still you've been set on getting me to go home at the same time as you!"

Grey looked down at his shoes. "I did notice all those things you said. I just pretended I didn't."

"Why?" Finn asked.

"Because I wanted to believe you would change your mind with enough time stuck here," Grey said. "You started to see some of the bad things, so I hoped you had finally gotten on board. I didn't want to leave you here. You're my best friend. How am I supposed to go to junior high without you?"

Finn smirked. "You'll be fine. You're tough after leading a squad in this crazy game. No way junior high could scare you now."

Grey frowned. "It wouldn't be the same without you."

"No, but . . ." Finn sat down. All the anger between them had fizzled quickly. Sadness was left behind, but also honesty. "It's not like I hate my life, okay? And it's not that I never want to go back. It's just that I want to be here a little longer. At least one more season."

"At least?" Grey kneeled down by his friend. "You seriously think you could do more?"

Finn nodded. "With a little more practice I could get home anytime I want. Just like Tae Min. I'm not afraid of being stuck here. The real world is scarier."

"Why?" Grey asked. While he could see the appeal of playing a video game all day, he couldn't understand not wanting to go back to the real world.

"First it's junior high. Then it's high school and college and getting a job and being a grown-up," Finn said. "We're twelve. In six years they expect us to be adults. I guess maybe I'm not ready to stop being a kid. This is like endless summer in here. I don't get why anyone would want to leave so fast."

Grey didn't agree, but he was beginning to understand why Finn wanted to stay. He wasn't doing a great job of convincing his best friend to come home. Instead, Finn was convincing Grey of his side. "Well, I wish you would have told me sooner that you wanted to stay here."

"You do?" Finn said in surprise.

Grey nodded. "I was so worried about leaving one of my friends here stuck. But if you *want* to be stuck here . . . I almost feel bad for making you rank up. You should go home when you want to. There are so many people who truly want those spots—it's not fair for you to take one if you don't even want it."

"That's true." Finn's eyes began to water, but he shook it off. "So you're not mad at me?"

"No. Maybe sad, though," Grey admitted. He

still didn't want to face junior high without Finn, but he'd rather face that than another season in this game. He didn't mind the idea of growing up as much as Finn did. "But we do need to tell everyone else the truth. It would be a lot easier to help Hazel if she was back in the squad."

Finn smiled. "Yeah, she'd like that."

"Tae Min will want to get her up to speed," Grey said. All this squad switching was exhausting, but Grey was certain this would be the last change.

"Maybe I can help still," Finn offered. "Kinda like Tae Min is."

"It could be good to split our numbers more," Grey said. "Let's talk it out with everyone."

"Sounds good." Finn smiled so wide that Grey knew Finn was happier to be here than Grey could ever be. That made it a little better.

Grey and Finn headed out to the practice area. Lam's squad would be somewhere out there, but Grey didn't want to deal with them. He sent Finn to find Hazel, while Grey went to let everyone else know the latest news. He found his friends outside another replicated Tilted Towers building. This was the big office building that stood off on its own in the northern part of the area.

"Where's Finn?" Kiri asked when he met up with them.

"He went to get Hazel," Grey replied.

Everyone but Tae Min gave him a confused expression. Tae Min only smiled. "Looks like I'll have some decent competition next season after all."

"Huh?" Ben looked between Tae Min and Grey. "Will you just tell us what's going on?"

Grey ran a hand through his hair. He knew Kiri would be fine with Hazel coming back, but Ben and Tristan might not be so welcoming. The last time they dealt with Hazel, she was still mean to all of them. "Well, it turns out Finn actually wants to stay in the game. With so many people wanting to get home . . . it doesn't seem right to get him in the top five."

Ben, Tristan, and Kiri all understood now, but they all had very different reactions.

Kiri smiled with relief. "That's why he was throwing, to help Hazel?"

Grey nodded.

Tristan looked like he'd smelled some stinky cheese. "I'm sorry, but she's not playing in our squad. I'd rather deal with Finn than her."

"Finn is stronger . . ." Ben looked down at his

shoes. "He'd round out our squad. If you want her back, she should be with you."

Kiri rolled her eyes. "She's not that bad. She's changed. You have to be flexible—we all do."

"Kiri's right," Tae Min said. "Hazel has sharp edges, but so do you, Tristan."

Tristan frowned but didn't argue.

Tae Min continued. "It's possible that the best team compositions will place Hazel with Ben and Tristan. I don't know yet, but once we practice I'll know what will work best. And having Finn floating between teams like I do will be good for everyone as well. This will only help you all get to the top five."

"We'll get over it," Ben said with a sigh. "This is about getting home more than anything else. Right, Tristan?"

"Right," Tristan replied.

Finn and Hazel appeared over the ridge. Finn waved and smiled. His energy had shifted to excitement now that he didn't have any secrets to keep. Hazel looked much more nervous. She walked with her arms folded. She bit her lip and looked at everyone like they might snap at her.

"Did Finn tell you?" Grey asked once they were close enough.

"She doesn't believe me!" Finn replied. "Like I would joke about something like this! I had to basically drag her here."

"How am I supposed to believe you'd take me back?" Hazel yelled over Finn. "I left you high and dry. You all said you weren't mad about it, but I figured that was only because Tae Min came to the rescue."

"We all know what it's like to be blinded by the game," Grey said.

Kiri came over and gave Hazel a hug. "Don't worry about it, mate. Let's do this together, ay? We want you to get home too."

"You punks are so . . ." Hazel hugged Kiri back as she began to cry. "Thanks."

"Okay, okay!" Finn made a sour face as he looked at Hazel and Kiri. "No more mushy stuff! Me and Tae Min gotta make sure you're in tip-top shape. Those top five spots aren't free."

Tae Min raised an eyebrow at Finn. "Why are you talking like we're some sort of duo?"

"Next season we should be!" Finn laughed. "We'd be unstoppable."

Tae Min shook his head. "Too boring. I need someone less easy to fight."

"Less easy?" Finn put his hand to his heart. "Ouch. You'll pay for that."

"No I won't." Tae Min turned to address everyone. "No more time to waste on talking. We need to get Hazel on track and figure out squads for tomorrow, not to mention finishing off studying Tilted."

"Let's do this!" Grey said. Maybe it wasn't the exact plan that he wanted, but if everyone was happy, then he was too. With everyone settled, they just had to take over the rest of the top five.

CHAPTER 7

Grey and his friends practiced every possible second that night and the next morning. As they gathered in a circle to discuss strategy for the day's battles, Tae Min put his hands on his hips and gave them all his scariest glare. Grey had learned that was just how he looked when he was strategizing, but it was still stressful.

"We need Ben and Tristan to take a couple more wins," Tae Min said. "I think adding Kiri in will help them most when we land in Tilted."

Grey nodded. "That makes sense. So it's me, Finn, and Hazel?"

"Yes . . ." Tae Min said. "With your more aggressive styles, I need you guys to take a risky mission."

"Ooh, what?" Finn said with excitement.

"You gotta find Lam's squad early," Tae Min said as he looked at Hazel. "Surely you know more about their landing strategies now."

"I do," Hazel said with a clever smile. "Lam picks the farming spot farthest from the bus path, but she might change it up because she obviously knows I will tell you stuff."

Tae Min nodded. "She'll still pick a low-population landing to farm. Do what you can."

Grey began to grow nervous at the thought of going after Lam's squad. Of course he and his friends would benefit from getting Lam's squad out early, but it also meant they could be eliminated too. "Are you *sure* that's the best plan? What if me or Hazel get eliminated early?"

"Hmm." Tae Min pursed his lips as he thought. "I will admit I'm not one hundred percent sure on the best plan here. I could duo with Finn and we could go after Lam's squad, but that would mean leaving you all to your own devices without any help."

"None of us can do Tilted Towers without you guys," Tristan pointed out. "Tae Min and Finn are the best at it."

"Right . . ." Grey let out a nervous sigh. "Well, I guess we will just have to see how it goes."

"Don't worry," Finn said as he slapped Grey on the back. "I'll take the hits if we get in a bad spot. Then you and Hazel can run."

"Yeah," Hazel said. "I've learned how to hide and box in from the pros."

That was true. Hazel had gained some valuable knowledge in her time away, so if anyone could outrun Lam's squad, it would be her. "So, we know Lam will land in an out-of-the-way farming spot, but should we go there too?"

Tae Min shook his head. "Take the best landing spot nearby, gear up, and then watch for them as they come in from the storm."

"Got it," Grey said.

Thirty seconds until the battles begin!

"Good luck," Tae Min said. "You got this."

"Yeah we do," Finn said. "We just have to find them."

"We will. Those top three spots won't be theirs for much longer," Hazel replied with determination.

They were all transported to the battle warehouse to begin the day. Grey and Kiri stood closest to Lam's squad, and Grey could feel the anger radiating from that side of the ranking line.

The Admin appeared with her cheery smile. Her suit was as pristine as ever, and her blonde hair was still styled the same way even after all these days. "Welcome to Day Fifty-Seven of Battles! There have been no reports. Please note that as the season comes to a close, the developers have determined not to implement any further changes in order to provide players with no unexpected alterations that may impede their gameplay and thus their rankings. We believe this is the fairest mode of action and wish our top players the best in their pursuit of victory. Good luck in today's battles!"

The countdown to the first battle began, and when Grey appeared in the Battle Bus, it was a little strange to only see Hazel and Finn in his squad. Kiri had been with him since nearly the beginning, and it felt weird not to have her sniper eyes to back him up.

"What's your best guess, Hazel?" Grey asked as he looked at the map. The bus was flying over the western side of the island, from south to north. It would be a great bus for his friends' landing in Tilted Towers.

"Hmm," Hazel said. Grey imagined she probably had the map open in her vision as well. "I'm gonna say Junk Junction. Lam likes being stocked on metal for her bases, and most people will probably land in the south."

"Sounds like a good guess," Grey replied. "So how about we try Pleasant Park?"

"Yes, please," Finn said. "Should be a good fight."

"Okay, going!" Grey jumped out of the bus with most of the other people. Everyone spread out in the sky, and he tried his best to observe where people were headed. There were lots that went to Tilted Towers as usual, but some went more south to Flush Factory and Greasy Grove. Some picked Snobby Shores and Shifty Shafts. Several seemed to be zoning in on Pleasant Park like them, but there were a few more headed north.

Three players caught his attention in particular, since they were gliding right for Junk Junction. Only two were headed for Haunted Hills. Grey had a feeling Hazel had guessed exactly where Lam would pick.

But Grey had to focus on the enemies at Pleasant Park first. Hazel and Finn picked separate houses, while Grey zeroed in on a gun that was on a gas station's roof. It glowed purple, and he knew by the shape that it was an SMG. That would be a great weapon to have first.

He had competition, though.

Another player swooped in next to him, and they landed at almost the same time. Grey dove for the SMG, hoping he would see it appear in his inventory. It did, and the player jumped off the roof before Grey could equip it and shoot. If this person wasn't giving up, Grey assumed he couldn't rest too easy.

The sound of a door opening below made Grey wait on the roof. There was probably a weapon in there, too, although he didn't hear the shimmering sound of a chest. His closest enemy was probably armed now.

Gunfire sounded from the other side of the soccer field, and Hazel lost half her health. "Shoot!"

"I got you," Finn said.

Finn eliminated Petra.

Grey decided he was in too vulnerable a position. Instead of pursuing the enemy, he jumped down from the roof and headed for the boxy house nearest to the soccer field. He needed more than just an SMG and a few bullets to survive.

Shots came from behind as he ran, and one hit him for just nine damage. The guy must have picked up a basic pistol with that low of damage.

Grey took one more shot before he got into the house. But luckily he could hear the sound of a chest nearby. He opened the closest door and, sure enough, there was a chest in there. He opened it—small shields, a trap, and a basic AR. He scooped them all up and used the shields immediately.

The enemy hadn't followed him. Grey assumed he'd probably gone somewhere else to find more loot.

"You guys okay there?" Grey asked. "I have one on this side."

"We're good," Finn said. "Think there's one more somewhere over here. They're lying low, though."

"We'll find them," Hazel said. "Focus on your prey."

Grey looted the rest of his boxy house. He didn't find a lot, but it wasn't too bad a haul. It would have been nice if he'd found a med kit to get his health back to full, but he wasn't that lucky.

There was a small gray house near Grey's

building, and he assumed that was where the enemy had gone. Both of them probably didn't have the best loot, but Grey had to be careful in pursuing this enemy. He had a feeling the player was good. Maybe one of the top twenty. This player didn't take a fight recklessly.

After getting as much material from the house as possible, Grey approached the gray house by building off of the roof. He wanted to keep the high ground, and as he landed on the gray house's roof, he stopped to listen for footsteps or the sound of a pickaxe swinging.

He could hear both.

But then it stopped.

Shots came at Grey from behind. He whirled around and spotted the source right before he boxed himself in. "This is a duo! His friend tried to get me."

"I see him!" Finn said.

Grey was sure that whoever had shot at him had warned his buddy that Grey was on the roof. Now the player would crouch and be quiet— Grey would have a much harder time finding him. He'd have to take the risk and push into the house.

Finn knocked down Yuri.

Finn eliminated Yuri.

"Careful, Grey!" Hazel called. "You have Vlad over there."

"Come back me up, guys," Grey said. Vlad would be careful now that he knew Grey's squad was there. There was a window just below Grey's position, and he jumped as he placed a floor right outside of it. He was immediately met with a shotgun to the face.

Vlad knocked you down.

"What the heck?" Grey yelled. He hadn't heard Vlad at all.

"We're almost there!" Hazel said as the sound of a tommy gun filled the air. It was comforting for Grey—Vlad wouldn't last through Finn and Hazel—but Grey had to avoid getting thirsted in the meantime.

Vlad aimed right for him, and Grey crawled to the side of his wooden floor hoping to drop down in time. But he moved so slowly. Vlad ran closer to get the right angle, but then he took damage and moved back. Grey was able to drop down onto the sidewalk as Finn and Hazel arrived from across the soccer field. Finn ramped up to take care of Vlad while Hazel built a box around Grey and began to revive him.

"Tsk. Get up, Pipsqueak," Hazel said.

Finn eliminated Vlad.

"Thanks." Grey was able to stand again. Hazel gave him a med kit, and he started using it to heal up.

But before he could finish, the sound of a rocket launcher blasting filled the air. The wall protecting Grey went down, and he had to move before the next rocket came. He and Hazel ran back toward the boxy house he had already looted.

"Three from the north!" Finn announced.

"It's Lam," Grey said as he took refuge in the house and tried to heal again. "She saw I was knocked down by Vlad and they guessed we were here."

"Vlad and Yuri do like the Pleasant drop," Hazel said.

"This is not good," Finn said. "We're barely geared."

Grey finally managed to get his heal off, but Finn was right—they weren't ready to face Lam's squad at all. Worse, if they were eliminated now, they'd be ranked in the sixties for this game. But they would have to fight, and they had to find a way to win.

CHAPTER 8

The rockets didn't stop coming. They pounded into the boxy house where Grey and Hazel were hiding. Grey had his good SMG and a few other decent weapons, but he was low on ammo all around. He didn't have much materials for building either. He needed to be careful.

"Any of you have C4 by chance?" Grey asked over the comms.

"I wish," Hazel said.

"No 'splodes here," Finn said. He was still holed up in the gray house. They would be coming for him any moment now. "No more time to think. I gotta fight. Back me up."

The crack of a shotgun started the fight, and Grey imagined Finn had raced right in. But so far there was no notification that he had been knocked down. Grey peeked out from behind a door in the broken building. Finn had his tommy gun out, and Lam's squad was using walls to protect from the spray.

Hazel took a deep breath. "C'mon, Grey. Let's make sure the others can get a good rank at least."

She had a point. While Grey wanted to survive, he was already in the top five. Barely. He needed his friends to keep ranking up—that meant hurting these top three players' standings. "Okay, let's go!"

Hazel led the charge, and Grey followed behind. They focused on the wall that Finn stood in front of, and this time it came down long enough for Finn to get another shot with his shotgun.

Finn knocked down Trevor.

"Nice!" Grey cried. But before he could react, Lam and Pilar focused their fire on Finn. His health bar went red immediately.

Lam knocked down Finn.

"Thirst Trevor!" Finn yelled. "Don't worry about me!"

Grey switched to his shotgun and aimed at

Trevor, hoping for once that the nerf to shotguns wouldn't make his damage too low. He fired and was relieved when Trevor turned into items. Grey spotted the glowing blue big shield potion, which he needed desperately if they survived this fight.

You eliminated Trevor.

One of the top three was now eliminated at rank sixty-one, but there were two more who had their aim on Finn. While Grey knew it was okay if Finn went out early, he still didn't like to watch it happen.

Lam eliminated Finn by head shot.

Now it was just Grey and Hazel versus Lam and Pilar. Normally Grey would have been defensive, but he didn't want to waste mats. Plus, he was angry. "Push them, Hazel!"

"Flanking!" Hazel called as Grey heard the sound of a bounce pad being used. Hazel flew above him, raining down shots on Lam and Pilar. "Hit both! No shields!"

"You guys got this!" Finn cheered as he watched from spectator mode.

Grey ran for Lam and Pilar head-on. They took aim, but he built a ramp not only to protect himself but to climb above them. Lam and Pilar were already boxing themselves in, and as Grey tried to break their roof, he heard the sound of a trap being laid. He backed off, not wanting to fall inside. He didn't have enough health to survive the dangerous trap spikes.

"Careful!" Finn said. "You guys are low, too. One explosive and—"

The suction sound of a clinger made Grey panic, but he didn't see one by him.

Hazel groaned. "It's on me. Backing away to hide."

The explosion went off and Hazel fell to her knees.

Pilar knocked down Hazel.

As Hazel crawled for cover, Grey turned back to the trap box where Lam and Pilar still stood their ground. Even this early in the game and with hardly any materials, they still loved to box in. It made Grey angry.

"Shoot at the trap wall," Finn called. "You got this, Grey. Don't give them time to heal!"

Grey equipped his SMG and unloaded the magazine on the box. He broke down one wall, which was when he noticed the ceiling was still open from when they first tried to trap him. Before Lam could replace the wall or the ceiling, Grey threw his own wooden wall up instead. He opened a window and aimed his building tool at the ceiling.

Lam and Pilar fired at him, and his health went down to ten. But he stood his ground so he could throw a trap on the ceiling. Once it was down, he frantically shut the window right before a fatal shot came his way.

Shwing.

The trap spikes came down, and the resulting notifications filled Grey with relief.

You eliminated Lam.

You eliminated Pilar.

"That was sick!" Finn said with a laugh. "If we were in the real world, a video of that play would go viral!"

"Can we not forget I'm almost dead over here?" Hazel said.

"Coming!" Grey ran to Hazel before he even looked at the loot from that epic fight. Hazel only had a few ticks of downed health left when Grey began reviving her.

Hazel let out a sigh of relief when she stood up. "Talk about cutting it close."

"It was my bad," Grey said as he and Hazel went back to pick over the loot. There were bandages and shields to help them heal up, plus a lot of weapons that were better than what they had. "Pleasant Park is a cruddy landing. We probably would have had better luck fighting them right at Junk Junction."

"They got lucky with their loot," Finn pointed out. "Freaking rocket launcher."

"But it's ours now!" Hazel picked up the rocket launcher.

"I'm taking the tommy gun," Grey said. Spamming wasn't the most elegant way to win, but he didn't care at this point. In a duo, they needed all the rapid fire they could get.

"Storm's coming," Finn said. "Better get moving."

And so Grey and Hazel did get moving. The rest of the game was fairly quiet, since they had already taken out two higher-ranked teams. Grey didn't want to make any more risky moves, and they waited it out until it was just them versus Ben, Tristan, and Kiri.

Grey and Hazel gave their friends the win, and when they all appeared in the battle warehouse again, Grey's eyes went right to the rankings board.

Grey was still in fifth and Hazel was in sixth.

But now Trevor had fallen to fourth place and Kiri was sitting in third.

"Ugh!" Trevor glared at Kiri. "Why can't you go home next season? This is the closest I've ever gotten!"

Kiri tipped her chin up. "Then you can go home next season."

"I don't have Tae Min easy mode to rely on like you do," Trevor spat back. "You guys all talk about playing fair, but how is this fair? He just picked you because he feels sorry for you—you're not actually any good. You don't deserve to go home!"

That struck a nerve with Kiri, and she began to tear up. Grey knew she never felt like she was very good at the game, even if she was now.

"She does deserve it!" Grey said.

"Stop being a sore loser," Hazel said.

Trevor rolled his eyes. "Traitors have no right to say that. You were crying about losing your spot just yesterday!"

Tae Min had fallen down in rank enough that it took him a moment to step into the argument. But once he did, everyone went quiet. "That's enough. For the record, I pick people with the most talent and the purest hearts. All of them have worked hard long before I came into the picture."

Lam was the one who stepped in now. "But you still came to the rescue, and that's not fair at this point. Why can't you just go home and stop acting like this game is your own personal kingdom?"

Tae Min raised an eyebrow. "I thought you wanted that top rank I gave up, but I can take it again if you'd like."

"You already are!" Lam threw her hands up. "You're just putting someone else in it. You think you're some good guy, but you're not."

"I never said I was the good guy," Tae Min said.

Lam looked like she wanted to fight for real, but she held herself back. "Someday, Tae Min, you *will* want to go home. And if I'm still here I will do everything I can to make sure you don't, just so you know how it feels. My squad has fought for this for so long! We've stuck together. We care about each other. You've kept us down this whole time just to help others get out."

"If you don't like it, report me," Tae Min said. "Again."

Grey's eyes went wide as this fight went deeper and deeper. He often forgot that others in the game had longer histories together. Hearing

Lam speak . . . Grey felt bad that Lam hadn't been able to go home yet.

"So the Admin can tell us all that your help is just 'teamwork' within a squad?" Lam shook her head. "No, thanks. Come on, guys. He's never gonna listen."

Lam's squad stomped away, leaving Grey's crew gathered in their wake. Tae Min smiled at Grey, but it didn't seem like a happy sort of smile. More like he was trying to hide his real feelings. "You guys pulled it off."

"Barely," Grey admitted.

"Whatever you did, it put Lam on tilt. That's hard to do." Tae Min looked over to where Lam was exiting. "Was your fight close?"

Grey nodded. "It could have easily gone the other way."

Tae Min's brow pinched with concern. "I see."

"Tae Min . . ." Grey was nervous to ask with so many people around, but he had to. "Is what we're doing really okay? Lam sorta had a point . . ."

"She's trying to get in your head. Don't let her. The end of the season is always like this," Tae Min said. "There is plenty of blame and anger to go around with so much on the line, but I don't control any of you. You are all using your own abilities to reach these ranks—don't let anyone tell you differently."

"Okay," Grey said, though he still felt bad. But he had a feeling that whoever was in the top ranks would be mad about losing them.

"Now, no more of this. Back to the real battle," Tae Min said. "Maybe we should reconsider our strategy again? We can't afford close calls."

Finn nodded. "I think we need you there. Just to be sure."

"Let's try it then. No reason to risk it all at this point," Tae Min said. "Another few wins and we should have Trevor out of top five by the end of the day, then Pilar, then Lam."

Hazel looked concerned. "It'll really take until the last day to knock Lam out of the top five?"

Tae Min nodded. "She's got a high average. We'll have to keep tanking their ranks for all of you to have a chance. The earlier we can find them, the better."

"Okay then," Hazel said. "I'd feel better if we outnumbered them. Even if we all lose out on Tilted Towers loot."

"I agree," Tae Min said.

The rest of the day went better with Tae Min

on the hunting crew. In the second game, Grey's squad was able to take out Lam's squad right at landing. They were placed in the nineties that game. The third game, Grey's squad got Lam's out in the eighties. And in the last two games, Lam's squad only made it to the seventies.

After the last battle, Grey looked at the rankings on the wall. Hazel had jumped back into the fifth rank behind Grey. Kiri had taken second, with Pilar at third now. Ben and Tristan were right behind Trevor. So close, and yet it still felt like it was so far away for all of Grey's friends to make top five.

This time it was Pilar breaking down in tears as they all stood there through the Admin's speech. She ran out right after, her squad mates right behind.

Grey cringed. "I really hate making people cry."

"I know, Pipsqueak," Hazel said as she patted him on the head. She pointed to her big smile. "But I'm smiling! That balances it out, right?"

"Yeah . . ." Grey looked over at Ben and Tristan, who still didn't look too happy. "I'd feel a lot better if we could all smile, though."

"We'll get there. I hope." Ben tried to grin,

but it didn't quite work. He was ranked right behind Tristan. If anyone was going to lose out, it would be Ben falling into the sixth spot at this rate.

After all Grey and Ben had been through this season, Grey couldn't let that happen.

CHAPTER 9

The adrenaline coursing through Grey was unbearable as he stood in the ranked line and waited for the Admin to appear. He couldn't believe it was the last day of the season. For so long it had felt like it would never come, and now that it was here, he wasn't ready for it.

But, as Grey feared, Ben was still in the sixth ranked spot. Grey and his friends had managed to knock Lam from the top into fourth place, but they only had five more games to get Ben in and Lam out.

It didn't feel like enough.

Grey would never forgive himself if Ben was marooned here when everyone else got to go home. Maybe Finn and Tae Min could help Ben get top five next season, but Grey didn't even want to think of that. Ben had been waiting nearly a year to go home. He was the one who helped Grey when no one else would. Ben was a good kid, and he deserved to finally escape this place.

"Welcome to Day Sixty of Battles!" the Admin said when she appeared. "This is the final day of the season. After the fifth and final battle, all rankings will be final. The top five players will be released from this virtual reality experience and returned to the physical world. For those staying, the patch for the next season will be put in place during your mandatory rest period, and we will welcome five new players tomorrow morning. Good luck in today's battles!"

Grey's vision went dark and then he appeared in the battle bus with the rest of the players. He tried to calm himself, but it didn't work.

There were only five more games left.

He and his friends had to get Lam's squad out as early as possible every battle, and even that might not be enough for Lam to fall two whole ranks. Grey was still in a squad with Tae Min, Finn, and Hazel. Tae Min had taken over the hunt for Lam's squad, and it had worked out pretty well.

"My bet is Lonely Lodge," Tae Min said, probably looking at the bus path on the map. "What do you think, Hazel?"

"It's a good bet," she replied. "There's that mansion over there on that side, too, out in the middle of nowhere. Lam likes that spot a lot."

"Then it's settled. Jump right when the doors open," Tae Min said.

The timer counted down the seconds, and the moment the back door opened, Grey leaped out into the sky. The first time he had to jump it scared him, but now it felt normal to fall through the air and soar on a glider.

They all aimed for Lonely Lodge, a remote area on the east side of the island. There was a big cabin there and a few other buildings amid the trees. A river ran through the area. It was like a nice camping ground, but there wasn't much loot, so people didn't usually land there.

But Grey saw three players gliding in the same direction. It was probably Lam's squad because they began to change direction to the mansion Hazel had mentioned.

"Looks like we found them again," Finn said as they all deployed their gliders. "Good way to start the day."

"Yeah," Hazel said. "Let's hope Kiri, Ben, and Tristan get just as lucky."

"I'll take the lookout tower," Tae Min said. "They won't push us; we'll have to go to them. Gear up."

"I'll go for the big cabin," Grey said. "Hazel, you come, too."

"Alrighty, Pipsqueak."

They glided to the roof of the cabin and began to break it down. Finn landed on a smaller building nearby. Tae Min flew onto the top of the giant wooden lookout tower right before Grey and Hazel got into the building.

Grey worked as fast as he could to loot and gather materials. They didn't have time to waste when they were on the edge of the island—and they'd have to go right to the cliff where the mansion was if they wanted to find Lam's squad. If the storm circle was in the west, they'd spend the whole battle running for safety. They had to find healing items otherwise they could be eliminated by the storm.

"Hurry, ten people are already down," Tae Min said.

"Just finished here," Hazel said as she and Grey grabbed the last of the meager loot. He was happy to have the tommy gun, but his shotgun was trash and the dual pistols weren't ideal. Hazel took the scar, the grenade launcher, and an LMG. They were lucky enough to at least find healing and shields.

"Time to find them," Finn said.

After a couple days of playing this hunting game, Grey's current squad had gotten quite good at it. They hardly had to speak about what was next because it was the same every time. While Lam had been a challenge to Grey, she wasn't one to Tae Min.

They found Lam's squad, took them out, and it all went smoothly from there for that battle. Ben, Tristan, and Kiri took the victory as planned.

When Grey appeared back in the battle warehouse, he saw that Lam had now fallen to the fifth rank. Tristan had jumped ahead to fourth. Ben was still in sixth.

"Ugh! I hate you all!" Lam stomped away without any argument this time. By now, there wasn't time for fighting outside of the battles.

Grey and his friends gathered together, and he looked at Tae Min. "What are we practicing now?"

Tae Min shook his head. "No more practice."

"What?" Ben looked concerned. "Why not? I'm still sixth!"

"You all have this down now," Tae Min said. "There's nothing more to teach. Today is about not letting the pressure get to us."

"And hoping Ben makes it," Tristan said.

"About that . . ." Tae Min folded his arms as he thought. "I think it's time to move Grey to your squad. Just to be sure. We've got Lam's number. Her squad members are starting to give up now that they've been knocked out of the top five."

That twist of guilt was still hard for Grey to move past. "Don't you think Hazel might be better? She's right behind me in rank and she'd be alone once you guys go out."

"I can handle myself," Hazel said. "They need me on the Lam hunting squad."

"We do," Tae Min said. "But also, your ranks are likely close to each other. Hazel held a higher rank than you for a lot of the season, so her taking the fifth spot in battle should be fine."

Grey nodded. "Okay, if you think it's good, then let's do it. Getting Ben in the top five is what matters right now."

"Thanks, guys, for trying so hard," Ben said as he looked down at his shoes. "Please don't feel bad if it doesn't work out, though. I know you gave it your best."

"You're coming with us, I promise," Grey said. He had to believe it himself if he wanted to stay focused. "Just one more spot."

Ben sighed. "Don't promise things you don't have control over. I know it's all in the rank averages now. It might not be enough."

"Don't give up yet," Kiri said.

"I'm not," Ben said. "I'm just trying to prepare myself in case I don't make it."

"That's not right," Finn said. "You gotta think positive, dude."

"It's not that . . ." Ben shook his head. "I need some time alone."

"You sure?" Grey didn't want to leave his friend to worry on his own, but Grey understood that sometimes people needed a break. Grey took many when he was stressed.

"Yeah." Ben walked off, probably to the forest many took solace in. He didn't come back until it was almost time for the next battle, and he still wasn't very talkative.

The next three battles went as they all

hoped—Grey, Kiri, Ben, and Tristan took the Victory Royales, and Hazel was able to hide out and take the fifth spot each time. Tae Min, Finn, and Hazel had found Lam early every battle. Lam was eliminated ranking in the eighties each time.

But still she remained in the fifth overall rank.

Grey couldn't believe it as he stared at the list in the battle warehouse. There was just one game left, and Ben was still in sixth place even after all those victories.

Lam let out a sigh of a relief. "Still in this."

She walked to a table to sit and wait out the hour before the last battle. Her teammates joined her, but Grey turned his focus to Ben.

"See?" Ben said quietly. Tears began to form in his eyes. "I knew it. I could feel it. I'm gonna be stuck here again."

"It's not over yet . . ." Grey said. "There's one more battle."

"If four victories didn't do it, how could one more help?" Ben turned to hide his crying.

"It could," Tae Min said. "Please don't give up now."

"I hate this," Ben said. "How am I supposed

to stay here another season when all my best friends are going home?"

In that moment, Grey wished he could trade places with Ben. He didn't think he could give up his spot, but suddenly it was all he wanted. Except it was impossible now. Even if Grey played badly and got a low rank in this game, he was ranked second. He wouldn't drop low enough to help Ben.

Could he ask the Admin to take Ben home instead?

He had a feeling it wouldn't work, but if the worst happened Grey might have to give it a try. Hopefully he wouldn't have to. They could all still get home if this battle went as well as the rest in the day.

Grey put his hand on Ben's shoulder, trying to be strong for his friend. "I wish I could trade places and it was me waiting in sixth, but it's not. We don't know what's going to happen. I'm sorry, but you gotta suck it up and play your best until the very end. We all do. Worrying about something that hasn't happened yet won't get us anywhere. All we can do now is fight for you and not think about the rest."

Ben's crying slowed, and he wiped at his eyes. "I'll try."

"That's all we can do," Kiri said as she stood at Ben's side. "I think it'll be okay. I can feel it in my bones."

"Why can't I?" Ben asked.

"Just rely on us to feel it for you," Tristan chimed in. "Grey always said he wanted to play to the end with us. And look, here we are, even after all the drama."

That made Ben crack a smile. "True."

"He also said we could make top five together," Tristan continued. "So let's believe it'll all come true. No one thought Grey was any good—"

"Wow, thanks," Grey said with a laugh.

"But they were wrong," Tristan said. "Grey worked hard and learned, and though he probably won't agree, he believed in himself this whole time. He would have given up weeks ago if he didn't. So if he believes we can all make it, then we have to believe it, too. He hasn't been wrong yet."

"No pressure or anything," Kiri added.

For some reason, that made Grey laugh and all the pressure in the group dissolved. Tristan was right—Grey wouldn't have said he had confidence in himself—but looking back on the entire season, he must have. Or at least he had enough to keep going even when it seemed impossible.

So Grey simply chose to believe Ben would make it until the very end. The last battle would determine everything.

CHAPTER 10

I t was the last time Grey would be sitting in the Battle Bus. After this, he would be able to go home, see his family, and get back to normal life. But he couldn't think of that yet—not until they won and he saw that Ben would get to go home too.

Grey took a look at the map to check the bus's path. It was flying east to west, almost right over the middle. "How about Fatal Fields, for old time's sake?"

"Sure," Tristan said.

"It feels like yesterday that I was eliminating you first on day one," Ben said.

"That was the most miserable day," Kiri chimed in. "I still can't believe Grey took me in."

"Was a good thing he did," Tristan said. "Now you're ranked first."

"Nuts, ay?" Kiri laughed. "It should be Grey."

"You have more eliminations by a lot," Grey said as the bus's door opened. "Okay, here we go!"

As Grey jumped out, he felt like he might miss the island after all. Maybe not the stress of competition, but he would miss his new friends. He would miss Finn until he decided to come back to the real world.

"I want the big red barn," Tristan called out. "Ben, come with me."

"Sure," Ben replied.

"I'll take the farmhouse," Kiri said.

"Then I'll grab the gray barn side." Grey smiled at the thought. That was the first place he ever landed.

There were several people landing with them, but Grey wasn't concerned. Most of the players were just messing around at this point. Sure enough, as Grey landed on the gray barn's roof, he watched the three players touch ground in the open field where they proceeded to start a dance party.

"Should I take them out?" Kiri asked. "I already have a sniper."

"Just knock one," Grey said as he opened his first chest. "Then we can know who they are. If it's not Lam's squad, leave them. If they're eliminated, that just helps Lam's rank."

"True," Kiri said. A loud sniper shot went off.

Kiri knocked down Guang.

"Hazel's old squad," Ben said. "They're reviving Guang in the open now."

"Leaving them to their dance, then," Kiri said. "They haven't even grabbed weapons."

Grey kept gathering his loot and materials, occasionally checking to make sure the dancers didn't decide to fight. They seemed harmless enough, but Grey wasn't about to get complacent now. He watched the notifications, waiting to see Lam's squad go down at the hands of Tae Min, Finn, and Hazel. It usually happened after looting the first area.

Lorenzo eliminated Martine.

Hans eliminated Dan.

Selena eliminated Mayumi.

From the looks of the quick succession of notifications, Grey guessed they were all in Tilted Towers. He hoped he'd see the eliminations he needed to see soon, because every minute that went by improved Lam's rank.

Lam knocked down Tae Min.

Grey froze in place as he read the notification in his vision again. That couldn't be right.

Lam eliminated Tae Min.

"Guys? I'm not hallucinating that notification, am I?" Ben's voice was already laced with fear.

"I see it, too . . ." Kiri said.

Finn knocked down Trevor.

Hazel knocked down Pilar.

"No . . ." Tristan's voice was a whisper.

Grey began to panic. He had no idea where they were, and even if he did, there was no way he could help his friends in time.

Lam knocked down Finn.

Lam eliminated Finn.

"What?" Kiri said. "This can't be happening! Did she find a full stack of C4 or something?"

"Maybe," Grey said. He tried to get a grip, but it was hard to focus when Finn and Tae Min were eliminated and Lam was still fighting Hazel. He hated that he couldn't even see what was happening, but he tried to remind himself that Tae Min was coaching Hazel. It could still turn around.

Hazel eliminated Trevor.

Hazel eliminated Pilar.

"Yes!" Kiri cheered. "Go Hazel!"

"It's not over yet . . ." Ben said. As they all waited to see what the notifications would say next, it felt like the suspense would never end. No other words came up in Grey's vision except:

The storm is moving in two minutes and thirty seconds!

"Did they both run?" Tristan asked.

"That's a good bet," Kiri said. "Shoot, Lam's still alive. Her rank will only go up . . ."

Ben let out a groan. "I'm doomed. I'm so doomed."

"Don't say that. Maybe Hazel will get her." Grey tried to shake off his worry about Ben as he looked at the map. The next storm circle was zoning in over the west side of the island. "We gotta move toward Shifty Shafts soon."

They started moving to the northwest, but Grey kept an eye on his notifications in hopes to see Hazel eliminate Lam. But the notification that came was worse:

Lam eliminated Hazel.

"Nooooooo!" Ben cried. He stopped right in the middle of an open area, and Grey hurried to build a box around them in case someone decided to take a shot.

"We can still win, Ben," Grey said as he tried to hold in his own panic. "Lam can't beat us all!"

"But her rank won't drop now . . ." Ben's avatar used the crying emote.

"It will, just not as much," Tristan pointed out.

Grey's mind raced through their options, and none of them seemed that great. They could just go forward and win the game—Lam would probably make it to the top five with her turtling skills. They could try to hunt Lam down—that could put them in a bad position if they focused too much on her. Or they could split up and do both—that would potentially make them weaker and they could lose the whole thing.

"We need to focus on how we can save this," Grey said. "The game isn't over yet."

"No matter what we do, we need better loot," Tristan said. "Maybe we should just go Tilted instead of Shifty."

"What does it matter anymore?" Ben sounded like he'd officially given up. "I'm staying here."

"No, you're not!" Kiri yelled. "Snap out of it right now, Ben. We're fighting until the very end, and I won't let you do anything else."

"Kiri's right," Grey said as he opened the box

and began to run. They still needed to get in the safe zone, and the storm was nearly upon them. "We gotta keep going, okay?"

"Fine," Ben said, though he sounded resigned.

As they approached Shifty Shafts, a plan formed in Grey's mind. It was risky, but he had to try for Ben's sake. "Okay, this is the best I've got. Since me and Kiri have the top ranks, I say we go after Lam and try to take her down. Tristan, you protect Ben and stay in the safe zone. What do you guys think?"

"I can do that," Tristan said. "But how will you find Lam?"

Grey sighed. "I've been hunting her for a few days, I'll just have to do my best guessing. My bet is she landed around Haunted Hills, since it's on the outskirts and was near the end of the bus's path. So she'll be moving south. We'll be moving north."

"We'd eventually meet in Tilted Towers," Kiri said. "It looks like the storm will be shrinking around there."

"Okay," Grey said. "Then that's the—"

Shots fired their way. Another pair of players was running toward Shifty Shafts from Greasy Grove. Tristan threw up walls, and Grey went into fight mode. Using ramps to get the high ground, Grey fired down on them. They blocked with a few walls of their own and began to build up as well.

By the way they used their materials, Grey was certain they were a good duo. He would guess it was Zach and Hui Yin by their aggressive style. "Protect Ben at all costs!"

"On it!" Kiri said as she fortified their position and built a tower. She fired two shots from her sniper rifle. "The pink-haired girl is one shot!"

"My turn!" Tristan said as he equipped his shotgun and pushed over the ramp.

Tristan knocked down Hui Yin.

"Get Zach!" Grey said as he unloaded his tommy gun on his enemy.

Zach didn't build or shoot at that point. He stopped and used an emote to bow before them. Tristan shot him once in reply.

Tristan eliminated Zach.

Tristan eliminated Hui Yin.

"Sweet revenge," Tristan said. "You and Kiri better get moving, Grey. You have a lot of ground to cover, and we're already down to fifty players."

"Right." Grey reloaded all his weapons.

Ben whimpered. "Lam's gonna get top five

this game. You can't just find her. She is the queen of turtling."

"Well, we have to try," Kiri said. "Because we want you to get home, too, Ben."

"Hang in there," Grey said. "Take it slow. Don't take a fight if you don't have to."

"You sound like Tae Min," Tristan said. "Go already! I got this!"

Grey and Kiri began their run, passing right through Shifty Shafts even though it looked like it hadn't been looted yet. They had to find Lam as soon as possible if they wanted to give Ben the best chance possible to make top five.

CHAPTER 11

As Grey kept his eyes out for any movement in the distance, he tried to think about where Lam might go after she eliminated Hazel. If she had really landed in the northwest area of the island, then the most likely spots were the soccer stadium, Snobby Shores, and Pleasant Park.

"Where are we going?" Kiri asked. "Not to be dramatic, but your choice sort of determines the fate of Ben's rank."

"I know." Grey also knew Ben could still hear him, so he forced himself to stay calm. "Lam's gonna be playing it super safe, so I bet she's at Snobby. It's remote, still in the circle, and she probably has her pick of loot."

"Sounds like the best choice to me," Kiri replied.

They headed for the houses on the west side of the island, which sat right near the ocean. The area was still neat and clean as if no one had touched it from the outside. But that didn't deter Grey. Lam was smart—she wouldn't touch anything on the outside because it would be suspicious.

"Let's split and check the houses," Grey said.

"I'll start at the north," Kiri replied. "Meet you in the middle."

"Perfect." Grey moved to the southernmost house and opened the door. Everything was still intact. Weapons still lay on the ground and not a single piece of furniture was gone. The chests still glowed, unopened.

The whole house was like that, so Grey grabbed the good loot and moved on to the next building. It was the exact same as the first. Since Kiri hadn't mentioned seeing anything, he began to worry he'd guessed wrong. Lam would survive longer, and Ben's ranking would be in more danger of staying at sixth place. They were now down to under forty players left. Grey had to hurry.

"Ben and I have to move to Tilted," Tristan said. "The storm is pushing us there."

"Yeah," Grey said as he looked at the storm timer. He and Kiri would need to get moving soon, too. "We'll meet you there. Hopefully after we find Lam."

Kiri arrived at the middle house about the same time as Grey. He opened the front door first, and his heart stopped when he looked up.

There was a trap on the ceiling.

"Kiri, look up," Grey said quietly, as if Lam could hear them.

"She's here," Kiri said in a whisper. "She has to be."

"We gotta be careful. That can't be the only trap," Grey said. "Lam always has a plan."

"She's already heard the door open. She knows we're here," Kiri replied as she equipped clinger grenades. "I picked these up in the other houses. I say we go in with a bang."

"Good idea." Grey used his AR to break down the trap. "You first."

Kiri walked inside and threw the grenades deeper into the house, then she backed out to avoid taking damage. The walls, floors, and ceilings broke from the explosions, and Grey held his shotgun at ready. His eyes waited to see movement, but there was still no sign of her.

That's when he heard the sound of building.

"Outside!" Kiri yelled as she ran back through the door.

Grey followed, and his jaw dropped as he took in the large ramp Lam was building. She must have gone through the back of the house. Grey almost shot at the ramp, but then Lam dropped a launch pad and flew into the sky on her glider.

Kiri and Grey opened fire, and Grey was able to hit Lam once as she flew. But then she glided over the mountain ridge and out of sight.

"She launched!" Grey announced. "We're following, but she's headed for Tilted."

"Of course she is," Ben said.

The storm is approaching!

The circle began to close on Grey and Kiri as they built up to the launch pad Lam had left for them. Grey jumped on it and flew into the air. To his surprise, shots flew his way. "She's trying to shoot us down! She's still on the mountain!"

That was when Grey realized Lam might not know who he was because he and Kiri looked like a duo at the moment. Grey changed his skins often, so it wasn't as if Lam would recognize him.

"She burned my shield!" Kiri said. "I might be in trouble."

"Hold on!" Grey said. "Tristan, Ben, build up from Tilted. She's on the north cliff and she doesn't know who we are. You could take her by surprise!"

"What if she shoots us?" Ben said. "I can't get eliminated now."

"You won't!" Grey insisted. "We have her surrounded!"

Lam began to build as Grey and Kiri got closer to landing by her. She knew they would soon have their weapons out. The moment Grey hit the ground, he began to build up in hopes to meet Lam at the top. Kiri built from another angle. Grey let off a round from his tommy gun, hoping to be enough of a distraction that Lam wouldn't spot Tristan and Ben on the other side.

"We have company in Tilted!" Tristan said as the echoes of gunfire in the distance filled Grey's ears.

"Lam first! Then we take care of them," Grey replied.

"Ben, you shoot Lam!" Tristan yelled. "I'll cover you!"

Ben let out a whine but said, "Okay, okay!"

Grey saw the extra fire come their way from the office building in Tilted Towers. Since he knew that was Ben, he pushed Lam harder without the worry of taking damage from the extra fire. Lam couldn't build fast enough to protect herself from every side.

Ben eliminated Lam by head shot.

"I did it!" Ben cried. "She's out! I'm probably still stuck here, but she's out!"

"We'll find out soon enough!" Grey said as he picked through Lam's loot. "There's a big shield for you here, Kiri."

"Good." Kiri picked it up and drank it. "Sounds like we have more fighting to do before this is over."

"Make sure Ben gets the most eliminations of the squad," Grey said. "He needs the first place."

As the storm circle got smaller, more people came to Tilted Towers, but Grey and his friends were prepared. They perched on the towers and took out the remaining players before they had a chance. Before long, they were the last ones standing.

Victory Royale!

Grey read the words over and over. It was the last time he'd see them in this virtual reality, and relief filled him from top to bottom. He did it. He was really going home.

Now they just had to wait one short teleport to see if Ben was going with them.

Grey's vision went black, and his heart raced as he waited to see the battle warehouse. This victory wouldn't feel right until he saw Ben's name in the fifth rank, and he hoped with every fiber of his being that it would happen.

When they appeared in their ranked line, Grey's eyes went right to the board:

1. Kiri
2. Grey
3. Hazel
4. Tristan
5. Ben

He blinked a few times to make sure he wasn't seeing things. That really was Ben's name in the fifth spot. That one last game had been enough to get him home after all. Grey's smile stretched his face so much it hurt.

"Yesssss!" Ben yelled at the same time that Lam cried, "Noooooo!"

The Admin appeared without any extra

fanfare. "We have reached the end of our season. Congratulations to those who have earned their way back to reality! You will have three minutes to say your goodbyes before your minds are returned to your physical forms. Good luck in your life's adventures. And to those staying, I will see you next season!"

The Admin disappeared, and Grey looked around him at all his smiling friends. "We did it, guys."

"We did!" Kiri said as she hugged Grey. "I'm gonna miss you, mate!"

"Thanks for everything, Pipsqueak," Hazel said as she ruffled Grey's hair.

Ben and Tristan both looked like they couldn't believe they were finally going home. Tristan said, "Thanks for helping us even when we didn't deserve it."

"And thanks for never giving up, even to the very end," Ben said.

"Thank you all for helping me," Grey said as he held back tears. Going home was still what Grey wanted, but he would miss these people he'd teamed up with for the last two months.

Tae Min and Finn arrived from farther down in the line, and a lump formed in Grey's throat.

It was one thing to say goodbye to his friends who were also going home, but it was different to say goodbye to his friends who were staying in the game.

"'Grats, dude," Finn said as he shoved his hands in his pockets. "You're gonna miss out on some sweet stuff in this next season."

Grey let out a laugh. "You'll have to tell me about it when you come back."

"I will," Finn relayed with a sad smile. "Promise."

Grey looked at Tae Min. "Make sure Finn doesn't stay forever, okay?"

Tae Min smiled. "Thanks for being such a good kid, Grey. You almost make me want to go back."

"I do?" Grey raised his eyebrows in surprise.

Tae Min nodded. "My faith in humanity has been restored a bit. Never thought that would happen. Never stop being yourself. The world needs kids like you."

"Thanks" was all Grey could say. Then his virtual body began to dissolve, and he felt a sinking feeling that his three minutes were nearly up. The battle warehouse as well as all his friends began to fade.

When he opened his eyes again, he was lying in a hospital room. His mom sat in a chair beside him. Her eyes were closed, and she looked like she'd been sleeping there for a long time.

Grey's eyes began to water. He really was back. He reached out a shaky hand and touched his mother's knee. She startled at the gesture and looked him right in the eyes. As the realization hit her, Grey smiled and said, "I'm home, Mom."

"You're awake!" His mother grabbed him into a hug, and he let her. He'd missed the sensation. "Are you okay?"

"I'm starving," he said. "Can I have pizza?"

His mother laughed. "I don't know. Let me tell the doctors you're awake."

Once she left, Grey took in everything about the room. He could smell again, even if it was a sterile hospital smell. He could hear the beep of the machines and the whirring of the ventilation. He could feel the weight of his body and the grumble of his stomach. It felt so good not to be in a video game.

But with everything he'd learned, he was ready to face his real life head-on. And he'd never take it for granted again.